The Corps of Discovery

CHARACTERS

Narrator 1

Narrator 2

President Thomas Jefferson

Meriwether Lewis

William Clark

Sacajawea

Chief Cameahwait

SETTING

Across America, from St. Louis, Missouri,
to the Pacific Ocean, 1803–1806

Narrator 1: The United States as we know it today stretches from sea to shining sea. A map of the country shows different states, bodies of water like the Mississippi River and the Great Salt Lake, and amazing places like the Rocky Mountains and the Grand Canyon. But let's step back in time more than 200 years. The country was still young. But it was growing.

Narrator 2: In 1803, the western border of the United States was the Mississippi River.

Narrator 1: In that same year, President Thomas Jefferson doubled the size of the country. He bought what was known as the Louisiana Territory from France.

Jefferson: At last, it seems possible that one day our borders will reach to the Pacific Ocean. We will be able to trade with the Far East. All this land, all these possibilities!

Narrator 2: No one really knew what kind of land lay beyond the Mississippi River.

Jefferson: To trade easily with China and India, we must find out if we can reach the Pacific Ocean by water. And if the people living on the land will be friendly to Americans.

Narrator 1: President Jefferson asked his old friend, Meriwether Lewis, to find out if there was an all-water route between the central United States and the Pacific Ocean.

Lewis: I would be honored. But I need someone to lead the journey with me.

Jefferson: I understand. This journey will be difficult. That is all we can be certain of. Who do you have in mind?

Lewis: My army captain, William Clark. He is not only brave, he is a talented mapmaker. He will make notes and drawings of the land, plants, and animals we find on our journey.

Jefferson: And, Lewis, it is most important that you build friendships with the tribes you meet on your journey west.

Lewis: You can be sure we will, sir.

Narrator 1: Lewis and Clark hired thirty men to join their group. They set out from St. Louis on the Missouri River on May 14, 1804.

Narrator 2: Lewis and Clark kept journals along the way. This is their story.

Clark: Because we are charged with exploring unknown territory, we call ourselves the Corps of Discovery.

Lewis: Our first five months on the Missouri River went well. We had peaceful meetings with the Oto and Yankton Sioux tribes.

Clark: We set up our winter camp among the Mandan tribe on the northeast bank of the Missouri River.

Lewis: Among the Mandan, we met a French-Canadian trader. He and his wife, Sacajawea, a native of the Shoshone tribe, wish to be hired as interpreters on our journey. We are grateful for their service.

Narrator 2: Sacajawea was to help Lewis and Clark communicate with Native Americans along the way. She would also guide the men across the land. She did all this while carrying her infant son with her.

Sacajawea: We will continue on the journey in the earliest days of springtime. I know the river and the land as well as I know myself.

Narrator 1: On April 7, 1805, the group left the winter camp.

Lewis: Away we go! I must say, getting back on the river today is one of the happiest moments of my life. Our men—and Sacajawea—are in excellent health and excellent spirits. We will reach the Pacific by fall. I can just feel it.

Narrator 2: In May of 1805, the group saw a great sight in the distance.

Clark: Lewis! Look, everyone! Look to the west. Do you see those incredible mountains?

Narrator 2: They were facing the Rocky Mountains. They did not know what to expect.

Narrator 1: This was not the only difficulty the Corps was facing. They had reached a fork in the Missouri River.

Lewis: I can't tell which fork of the river is the Missouri. A wrong turn might delay our journey by a whole season.

Sacajawea: We must cross a great falls before we reach the mountains. Whichever direction leads to the falls will be the correct way.

Clark: Clear water usually comes from the mountains. So I suspect the clear-flowing fork of the river is the way.

Lewis: Just to be sure, let's explore each route. We'll split up. Keep your ears open for the Great Falls. If they are as great as their name, the noise from the waterfall should be quite loud.

Narrator 1: Clark's group went one way, Lewis's the other. Soon, Lewis heard a noise.

Lewis: I hear the roaring of water. The spray rises like smoke in the air. This must be the Great Falls! This is our route!

Narrator 2: A messenger set off to let Clark know that the falls were found.

Lewis: These falls are the greatest sight I ever beheld. Amazing!

Clark: Well done, Lewis. Now how are we going to get ourselves and our gear around these raging waterfalls?

Lewis: We will have to carry our boats.

Clark: Up those steep cliffs?

Lewis: I see no other way.

Clark: Neither do I. Let's go.

Narrator 1: The journey was hard. In their journals, Lewis and Clark wrote of crossing the falls.

Lewis: There are great numbers of dangerous places. The men are weary, hauling the boats up sharp rocks and around slippery slopes. There are rattlesnakes everywhere.

Clark: At one point, we had to take shelter from a strong storm. Rain and hail made it impossible to go on. While in our shelter, a great torrent of water rushed toward us. We escaped the water, but lost some of our gear.

Narrator 2: The trip around the falls took 11 days.

Sacajawea: Now that we are beyond the Great Falls, the mountains will soon be upon us.

Lewis: How long do you think it will take to get past these mountains? Two days? Three days?

Sacajawea: No. The range is much larger than you can imagine. It will take many, many days.

Clark: Our team cannot carry our gear up and down steep slopes again, like we did at the Great Falls. Not for such a long journey. To have any hope of crossing the mountains successfully, we will need horses.

Lewis: Horses! Where will we get horses?

Clark: Sacajawea, what do you suggest?

Sacajawea: This land looks familiar to me. I am quite sure this is the land of my own people, the Shoshone. We must find them. They have horses. We may be able to trade with them for the horses we need.

Lewis: I hope so. If we cannot get horses, we cannot cross the mountains, and our journey will be in danger of ending too soon. We cannot go back to Washington without reaching the Pacific Ocean. We won't!

Clark: No. We will trade goods for horses. It's as simple as that.

Narrator 1: It wasn't quite so simple, though. Lewis and Clark had met many tribes on their journey. So they were low on goods to offer the Shoshone. Still, they had no choice.

Sacajawea: Look, on the ground ahead. Those are horse tracks. That means we are near the Shoshone.

Lewis: That's good news. Clark, you and Sacajawea take a group to look along the river for the Shoshone. I'll take a team to look on land.

Narrator 1: Lewis's journal told of meeting the Shoshone.

Lewis: My group found the Shoshone first. We did as Sacajawea said, so even though the Shoshone didn't seem to trust us at first, they soon learned we were friendly. Chief Cameahwait invited us to a tribal meeting when Clark arrived.

Narrator 2: When Clark and Sacajawea did arrive, Sacajawea did a dance of joy.

Sacajawea: These are my people! My first tribe!

Clark: Wonderful! This will help us at our meeting with the chief tonight. Sacajawea, are you ready?

Sacajawea: Yes, I am ready. I will have plenty of time to catch up with my old friends before we go. Now we must speak with the chief about the horses we need.

Lewis: Let's go, then. Right in here. Sacajawea, please introduce Clark to Chief Cameahwait.

Sacajawea: Cameahwait! I can hardly believe my eyes! It is you, my own brother!

Cameahwait: My own sister, who was taken from us? You have grown into a lovely woman! Welcome back to your first home, Sacajawea.

Sacajawea: Thank you! I am happy to see you, but my new home is a good place.

Cameahwait: Has your new tribe treated you well, Sacajawea? Are you happy?

Sacajawea: Yes, brother. I am happy. I have a husband and a son. And I have been helping these captains, Lewis and Clark, on their journey to the ocean.

Cameahwait: I am impressed that you have grown into such a leader. Now, let us get to the business that you wished to discuss. What is it that you need from our tribe?

Lewis: We need horses, but I'm afraid we don't have much to offer in return. We will trade what we have, but I can also promise that American traders will be back this way in the future. They will supply you with what you wish.

Cameahwait: Then it's settled. But know that crossing the mountains will be very challenging, even with horses. The land is harsh, and there is little food. But once you are past the mountains, you will be just a three rivers' journey from the ocean.

Sacajawea: Thank you, brother. The tribe has been very kind.

Narrator 2: It took the group about three weeks to cross the Rockies. The trip was difficult. The horses were always in danger of slipping down the steep mountains. When it wasn't snowing, it was raining. The group couldn't find game to hunt. They shot and ate some of their colts.

Narrator 1: Once past the Rockies, the course was easier. Up to this point, the Corps of Discovery had rowed against the stream. But past the mountains, the rivers flowed west toward the ocean.

Narrator 2: The Corps of Discovery traveled three rivers. The last one brought them to the Pacific Ocean. The men's journals tell of reaching their goal.

Clark: Ocean in view! Oh, the joy! At last. The Pacific Ocean.

Lewis: As we reached the ocean, Captain Clark marked on a large pine tree: "Captain William Clark, December 3, 1805. By land. United States in 1804–1805."

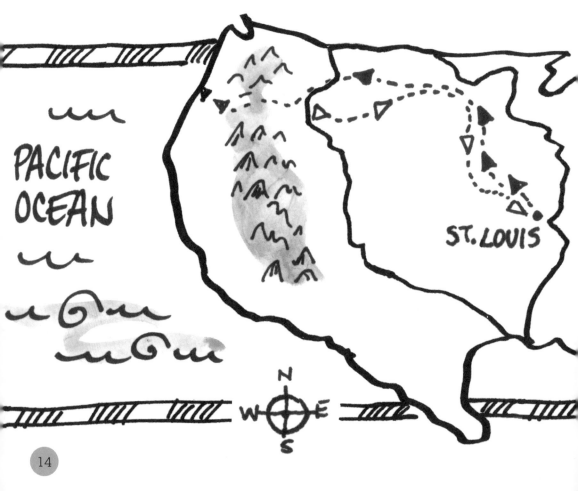

PACIFIC OCEAN

ST. LOUIS

Clark: I wrote "by land" because we now knew that there is no all-water route to the ocean.

Lewis: We spent the winter in a camp near the ocean. Then it was time to head back. We retraced part of our journey, but split up to explore more of the land.

Clark: Our journey had lasted two years, four months, and ten days. We had traveled about 7,000 miles.

ATLANTIC OCEAN

KEY
◄--- JOURNEY WEST
---▷ RETURN HOME

Lewis: I sent a letter ahead to President Jefferson: "It is with pleasure that I announce to you the safe arrival of my party today. We have crossed the continent of North America to the Pacific Ocean. We discovered the most practical route that exists across the country. Clark and I see this route as being good for trade."

Jefferson: Lewis and Clark have entirely fulfilled my expectations. The world will always admire their accomplishments.

Narrator 1: Lewis and Clark proved that there is no all-water route to the Pacific. But they showed that such a journey is possible between water and land. They opened the way for trade. They mapped the western frontier. They found 122 animals and 178 plants that Americans had not known about. They inspired others to follow.

Narrator 2: In the end, the incredible journey of the Corps of Discovery helped shape a country that would indeed now reach from sea to shining sea.

The End